# THE ADVENTURES OF
# PELICAN PETE

## A BIRD IS BORN

PICTURES BY HUGH KEISER
VERSE BY FRANCES KEISER

*Happy Adventures!*

Sagaponack Books • Saint Augustine

## We wish to acknowledge the following experts for their accuracy checks:

- James A Rodgers Jr., Biological Scientist IV, Wildlife Research Laboratory,
  Florida Game and Freshwater Fish Commission; Gainesville, Florida
- Dale Shields, "The Pelican Man," President and Founder
  Pelican Man's Bird Sanctuary; Sarasota, Florida

## Thanks to all who gave their time, advice, opinion, expertise, and encouragement:

Jim Collis, Gail Compton, Mike Crocker, Jeannette Crockett, Matt and Tara Dunn,
Frank Greene, David and Kerry Hadas, Dana Haden, Cathy Hagen, Kathy Kahnt,
Harry Kelton, Darlene Kelton, Erin Knight, Carl McNeal, Steve and Dena
Meyerhoff, Nick Mirkis, James Rodgers, Jim Runyeon, Sue Ann Russum, Dale
Shields, and Ruth Van Giezen.

Publisher's Cataloging-in-Publication
*(Provided by Quality Books, Inc.)*

Keiser, Hugh.
    The adventures of Pelican Pete : a bird is born / pictures by Hugh Keiser ; verse by
Frances Keiser. — 1st ed. p. 32. cm. 26.
    SUMMARY: A story in rhyme about a pelican egg which hatches into curious young
Pete. To protect his head from the sun, his parents find a child's cap for him to wear.
    Audience: Ages 4-8.
    LCCN: 98-96902
    ISBN: 0-9668845-0-7

    1. Pelicans—Juvenile fiction. 2. Pelicans—Eggs—Incubation—Juvenile fiction. 3.
Eggs—Incubation—Juvenile fiction. 4. Stories in rhyme. I. Keiser, Frances. II. Title.
III. Title: Pelican Pete.

    PZ8.3.K273 Ad 1999      [E]
        QB198-1755

For
Jeremy, Nicholas, Hannah, Cassy,
Tyler, Raeanne, Jason, and Sierra

For all the children good and sweet:
I'll tell a tale of Pelican Pete;
And for all who were *bad* today:
I'll tell the story anyway.

Pete's a bird who's fun to know,
Having adventures high and low.
So let's join Pete and follow his trail
From the beginning, where we start our tale...

As weather warms in early spring,
When flocks of migrating birds take wing,
Two courting pelicans chance to meet
And choose each other: life's complete.

Then, on an island near the sea,
With lots of birds for company,
They build a nest, twig by twig,
Until just the right size and not too big

For three large eggs of chalky white
That snuggle together, nice and tight.
Pete's in one, his sister another;
The third contains little brother.

Mother and Father are always there,
For eggs require lots of care.
Taking turns day and night,
They keep the temperature exactly right

By sitting with their large webbed feet
Covering the eggs to keep the heat
Perfect for the chicks to grow:
Not too high and not too low,

And guarding them from man or beast,
Who'll steal the eggs for a tasty feast.
So, here's a lesson you must know:
Near an occupied nest one shouldn't go,

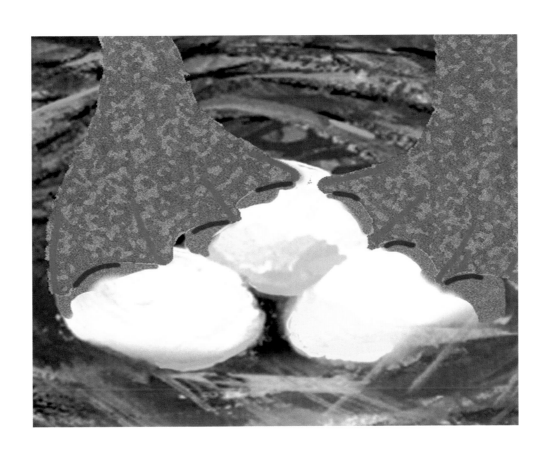

Because eggs and babies are easy prey
If their parents are frightened away,
Leaving them open to any foe —
Like wily, crafty, and cunning Fish Crow,

Who in the distance likes to wait
For unaware people to create
A disturbance at the nesting tree,
Making all the birds panic and flee.

Oh no! The eggs are unprotected!!
And, of all the nests, Crow has selected
The one with Pete to raid and attack —
A pelican egg for his mid-day snack.

Oh, what will happen to poor little Pete
As Crow flies closer with outstretched feet?
He'll peck his shell and, with a sharp beak,
End Pete's life of less than one week.

But just as Crow is inches away,
Mother and Father save the day:
Chasing him with long bills snapping;
Enormous wings, flapping and slapping.

Crow won't return any time soon;
They drive him away, over the dune,
Beyond the river, and past the shore.
The nest is safe and secure once more.

It takes thirty days for Pete to grow
Big enough to make a show,
To break his shell, to enter the world:
A tiny chick, all wet and curled.

He's not very cute, soft, or cuddly;
He's naked, gray, and downright ugly!
Having no feathers to shade his skin
In the open nest on a low tree limb

What a sunburn he would suffer
Without his parents there for cover.
But Pete is such a curious guy,
Popping his head from the nest to spy

All around, to his parents' regret,
Who worry and puzzle and start to fret.
His head will burn in the very hot sun:
Their sweet little babe won't make age one!

To each other they convey:
"We must do something. We can't delay."
"What can we do? That chick will *never* learn
To cover his head so it won't burn."

"Wait a minute! I have a thought.
High on that branch the wind has caught
A little blue cap, lost by a child,
And without much effort it'll be styled

Into a perfect cover for his head so dear;
Then sunburned skin we'll no longer fear."
"A great solution for the problem at hand,
And on our son, it will look grand!"

Pete loves having a hat of his own,
And to all his friends it is shown.
Whether he's in the air or on the ground,
On his head it's always found.

So across the land, far and near,
To this day, you will hear,
"There goes Pete, I can tell in a snap;
He's the only pelican wearing a cap!"

Now that Pete has left his shell
He's ready to learn his lessons well:
The things a baby bird must know
To help him live and help him grow.

He needs the skills to fly and eat,
To keep his feathers clean and neat.
There's so much to learn, discover, and see
With a nod, Pete beckons, "Come along with me!"

# Did You Know?

- There are seven species of pelicans in the world. Two species live in the United States: the white pelican and the brown pelican.

- The brown pelican's scientific name is *Pelecanus occidentalis*. They are playful birds with plenty of personality.

- In captivity, brown pelicans have been known to live for more then 30 years; in the wild, they may live beyond 20 years, but only 2% make it to the age of 10.

- Brown pelicans live along the seacoast. They build their nests on islands, either in trees or on the ground.

- Egrets, herons, and cormorants are some of the other birds who share the nesting colony. The nests are built close to one another.

- During courtship, the feathers on the heads of mature brown pelicans turn golden, the skin around their eyes turns bright pink, and their eyes turn blue.

- The male pelican picks the spot he wants to build a nest and then attracts a mate. The female builds the nest from sticks and small branches he brings to her.

- The female lays from one to four eggs, and both she and her mate take turns keeping them warm.

- Pelicans use their feet, which have many warm blood vessels, for incubating the eggs.

- Gulls, vultures, and ravens, as well as fish crows, will prey on untended eggs and chicks.

- A pelican is born without feathers and looks more like a dinosaur than a bird. The pink skin turns a purplish gray within 24 hours.

- Until they grow their first downy feathers, baby pelicans are shaded from the sun and sheltered from the cold by their parents. This is called brooding and the babies would not survive without it.

- Wildlife care facilities send volunteers to rescue abandoned, injured, and orphaned birds and to care for them until they can be returned to the wild. Do you know who to call if you find a bird in need of help?

## To Learn More About Pelicans:

Pelicans are social birds and enjoy spending time together. Go to the places where pelicans like to gather to see them up close. They have become accustomed to people watching their antics at locations such as piers, bridges, and docks where people go regularly to fish. But remember: don't feed wildlife.

Be a guest of a wildlife rehabilitation center. Many are open to the public; others require an appointment. These facilities care for injured birds, many of which can't be returned to the wild and become permanent residents. To locate the centers in your area, consult the "Wildlife Rehabilitation Directory" on the internet or call your state's natural resource agency. This agency will have Fish and Game, Conservation, Natural Resource, or Wildlife in its title. You may also locate state agencies and wildlife refuges and sanctuaries through the U.S. Fish and Wildlife Service's web site.

Visit your local library or book store for books on pelicans. Some very good ones are: Pelicans, by Dorothy Hinshaw Patent; The Pelican, by Lynn Stone; Wonders of the Pelican World, by Joseph Cook and Ralph Schreiber; and Florida's Fabulous Waterbirds: Their Stories, by Winston Williams.

Surf the Web. There are many sites about nature on the internet. A good place to start is the National Wildlife Federation or the U.S. Fish and Wildlife Service. Yahooligans.com, a web guide for children, lists other science and nature sites. Additional links may be found at the Pelican Pete web site – www.PelicanPete.com.

## About Sagaponack Books

Sagaponack Books publishes children's books to support Earth's beauty, habitats, and wildlife for continuing generations by helping children understand the natural world and foster a desire to protect it.

To learn more, visit our website at www.SagaponackBooks.com

Hugh Keiser, a graduate of Cooper Union, has been painting and drawing for over forty years. His work, the recipient of many awards, is included in numerous public and private collections.

Hugh began to explore the computer as an art medium about the same time he and Frances moved to Florida and fell in love with the brown pelican: the clown prince of birds. Illustrations for a series of books featuring Pelican Pete are the result.

Frances Keiser, naturalist, wildlife rescue volunteer, and friend to animals and children, has worked for the public school system with preschoolers and conducted children's craft workshops.

Raised on fairy tales, Frances continues to develop her love of children's books by being a collector and avid reader to children. Many of her favorite stories are in rhyme, which influenced her to write her own books in verse.

*The Adventures of Pelican Pete* books are an accurate and educational depiction of nature, historic and geographic locations, and wildlife Included in each story is a lesson to aid the safety of our wildlife or environment.

Living on the beach near St. Augustine, Florida, the Keisers' home is aptly named "Pelican Perch."

ل